THE ADVENTURES OF BEAST

Beast
Has a Party

Beast
Has a Party

Written & Illustrated By
Sheila Sanders

Edited By
Marjorie Oelerich
Professor of Early Childhood & Elementary Education
Mankato State University

BAKER STREET PRODUCTIONS, LTD.

502 Range Street, P.O. Box 3610, North Mankato, MN 56002-3610, U.S.A.

LIBRARY OF CONGRESS CATALOGING IN PUBLICATION DATA

Sanders, Sheila.
  Beast has a party.
  (The Adventures of Beast)
  SUMMARY: Beast gives a party with his friends to welcome Hyena to the neighborhood, but when Hyena arrives he is so rude, no one wants to know him.
  (1. Monsters--Fiction. 2. Animals--Fiction. 3. Friendship-Fiction.) I. Oelerich, Marjorie L. II. Title. III. Series: Sanders, Sheila. Adventures of Beast.
PZ7.S19788Bdd   1987   (E)   87-966
ISBN 0-914867-16-4

International Standard Book Number:	Library of Congress Catalog Card Number:
0-914867-16-4	87-966

Beast decided to have a party for Hyena, who had just moved into the neighborhood.

He called his friends and said, "I'm having a party for Hyena. Would you like to come?"

Rabbit said, "I'd love to! And I'll bring some punch."
Pig said, "I'd love to! And I'll bring a cake."
Kangaroo said, "I'd love to! And I'll bring ice cream."
Bear said, "I'd love to! And I'll bring party hats."
Frog said, "I'd love to! And I'll bring some games."

Beast called Hyena.
"I'm having a party for you to meet my friends.
Would you like to come?"

"Well," said Hyena, "will you have punch, and cake, and ice cream, and party hats, and games?"

Beast thought this was rude, but he said, "Yes, we'll have all those things."

"Good," said Hyena.
"Then, I'll come."

The day of the party came.
Beast and his friends got everything ready.

Then they waited for Hyena.
They waited, and waited, and waited.

Finally, the door opened, and in walked Hyena.

"Boy, am I thirsty!" said Hyena.
"I want some punch!"
Then he picked up the bowl, and drank all of the punch!

"Boy, am I hungry!" said Hyena.
"I want some food!"
Then he ate half of the cake, and all of the ice cream.

"Is this my party hat?" asked Hyena.
"I want the green party one."
Then he took the green hat from Bear's head.

"Let's play this game," said Hyena.
"I want to be first."
Then he started to play. He let no one else have a turn.

"I have to go," said Hyena.
"I'll see you later."
And he left.

Beast and his friends looked at each other and said,
"What a **rude** Hyena!"

The very next day, Hyena saw Rabbit jumping rope.
"Let me jump rope," said Hyena.
"Sorry," said Rabbit. "I have to go now."

Then Hyena saw Pig shooting baskets.
"Let me shoot baskets," said Hyena.
"Sorry," said Pig. "I have to go now."

Then Hyena saw Kangaroo and Bear playing croquet.
"Let me play croquet," said Hyena.
"Sorry," said Kangaroo and Bear. "We have to go now."

Then Hyena saw Frog playing marbles.
"Let me play marbles," said Hyena.
"Sorry," said Frog. "I have to go now."

Then Hyena saw Beast.
"Your friends are mean," said Hyena.
"No one will play with me!"

"That's too bad," said Beast.
"But they think you are rude."
"That's crazy!" said Hyena.
"What did I do?"

"Well," said Beast, "at the party,
you came very late,
you drank all the punch,
you ate half of the cake, and all the ice cream,
you took Bear's party hat, and
you played the game without taking turns."

"That's rude?" asked Hyena.
"But the party was for me!"

Hyena went home.
He sat all alone and thought.

Then he called Beast, and Rabbit, and Pig, and
Kangaroo, and Bear, and Frog.

And the next day, they all went to Hyena's house for
another party.

At this party, Hyena was not a bit rude.
Everyone ate cake, and drank punch, and took turns
playing games.

Hyena told jokes so funny that they all rolled on the floor and laughed until their tummies were sore.
It sure is nice to have friends!

THE ADVENTURES OF BEAST

If you
enjoyed this book,
you should read
the other books
in the Beast series.